ADIANNA

&

THE TOAD

A Story of Growth, Empowerment,

&

Letting Go
A Book for Girls
8-11

by

CC Wellington

When you help others, remember to take care of yourself, too.

Fill your own cup so you can shine even brighter!"

Be Your Own Best Friend!

Thank You

Long, long ago, in a far-off land in a far-off time, in the crystal-clear waters of the Caribbean Sea, there was a tiny magical island called Ekuo. It was there that the beautiful Princess Adianna lived, surrounded by coconut trees, mango groves, and palm trees.

Adianna, with her soft, curly hair wrapped neatly in braids and her gentle brown eyes, was a kind and capable princess, always working hard and doing special things for the people in her life. She took care of everyone.

One day, as the Princess swam in the aqua-blue sea, she heard a low, gravelly voice crying out, "Help me, please! Can you help me?" The voice pleaded desperately.

Curious and concerned, Adianna swam to the shore, and there, nestled among the fragrant flowers of vibrant hibiscus and cascading bougainvillea, was a toad. A pale, sickly toad.

 "Help me. You must help me. Please!"

Adianna knelt beside the sick toad with its massive protruding eyes and mottled, pale, clammy skin. It broke her heart to think that any creature could suffer in such a beautiful place.

Her heart swelled with compassion as she picked up the little yellow toad and kissed it gently as if her kiss could make it better.

"Oh, you poor thing," she whispered. "Don't worry, I'll take care of you."

The toad's lips curled into a weak smile. "Thank you," he croaked. "No one has ever cared for me before." He smiled sweetly as she started to make her way back to the palace.

Mixing different potions of healing herbs, tonics, and tinctures, Adianna lovingly cared for the toad, nursing him back to health. She even built him a beautiful cage in the lily pond next to the palace garden.

The toad grew stronger day by day.

"You are so kind, Princess," he would say. "Without you, I would have perished."

Adianna would smile warmly. "I'm happy to help. We all need care sometimes."

But over time, things began to change.

You see, as Mr. Toad grew bigger and stronger, he began to change in more ways than one. His once-yellow, splotchy skin now rippled with unseen currents. He no longer appreciated Adianna's kind, caring manner towards him. The small, sickly toad had grown to be large and toxic.

Day after day, the royal subjects could hear him screaming and yelling at the princess.

"Go away!"

"Fetch me water!"

"Bring me something else to eat!"

The once sweet and energetic Adianna became tired and sad as all her energy was focused on trying to please the now toxic toad.

Adianna's once bright and cheerful spirit began to dim. She became tired, drained from doing everything she could to please the toad. Neglecting her royal duties and avoiding her family and friends, everyone began to talk about Princess Adianna and the toxic toad.

Trapped by the Toad

One evening, as the sun set over the turquoise waters, Adianna sat beside the pond, watching the toad with sad eyes. He no longer seemed like the poor creature she had once rescued. His once pitiful cries for help had transformed into sharp, cruel commands.

"Why do you keep me here, Toad?
You are so unkind," she asked softly.
"I've done everything I can for you, but
you're always angry with me and
you always want more."

The toad's eyes flashed with something cold and dark.

"Of course, you should stay beside me," he replied. "Without me, what would you do? You've spent all this time caring for me—don't you see? You need me as much as I need you."

For the first time, Adianna felt a chill run through her. Something wasn't right.

As the days turned into weeks, Adianna began to feel as if she was shrinking inside. She no longer saw herself.

"What am I to do?" she cried every day. But there was no answer.

After a particularly poisonous argument with the toxic toad, Adianna sat in the mango grove and cried helplessly.

"Is there no one who can help me?"

the princess wailed.

It was on this day that she came across the gardener quietly digging away at the weeds surrounding her favourite mango tree.

"I've never seen you before," she whispered.

She sniffed slightly, embarrassed that the gardener saw her tears.

"I've always been here, your Grace, you just never called out for help before." "My name is Migara," the gardener said, introducing himself, "I tend to the weeds in your garden."

"I'm sorry," the princess sobbed bitterly, "I have been so preoccupied I never noticed you before."

Overwhelmed, she began to tell Migara the whole story of her relationship with the nasty, toxic toad and how he had taken over her life.

"I just can't make him happy," she cried. I don't know what to do."

Migara looked at the princess with a warm and understanding smile. His voice was soft but clear when he spoke.

The Magic

"Your Grace, if I may, sometimes we care so much for others that we forget to care for ourselves.

If your compassion does not include kindness to yourself, then you are incomplete."

Taken aback by his direct statement, the princess became angry.

"How dare you speak to me in that manner!" she chided, "You are becoming far too familiar."

Migara's deep brown eyes pierced into hers. For a single moment, the princess glanced away, unable to bear the intensity of his observant gaze.

"Your Grace, if you keep telling yourself the same sad story, you will always be stuck in it," he continued.

"Who do you think you're talking to?" the princess chided. "I am Princess Adianna of Ekuo! You are the gardener and you are crossing a line."

"I'm glad you're angry," Migara continued, "maybe this anger can motivate you to do something different about your sad situation."

Your Grace, if you keep telling yourself the same sad story, you will always be stuck in it.

Adianna jumped to her feet and turned to rebuke the gentle gardener again, but he was no longer there.

Try as she might, she couldn't find him anywhere.

"Where is the new gardener?" she yelled as she ran through the mango grove.

"Where is Migara?"

But no one knew who he was. According to the other servants, there was no new gardener.

Now left with her feelings, the princess began to question her thoughts.

Who was the mystery gardener who had given her this powerful advice?

Could what he had said be right?

Where did the gardener come from?

Confused with so many unanswered questions, Adianna turned her feelings inward and began questioning herself.

As she questioned herself, she became more frustrated.

As she became more frustrated, she started to feel angry.

But who was she angry with?

Was she angry with Migara?

Was she angry with her situation?

Was she angry with herself?

The sun began to set as she
pondered these thoughts.

That night, she sat by the pond, watching the toad as he lounged in his lily-pad cage. "Toad," she began, her voice steady and calm. "It's time for you to leave."

The toad's eyes widened. "Leave? You can't make me leave! You need me!"

Adianna shook her head.

"No. I don't. I cared for you when you were weak, but now I see that you've become strong—and with that strength, you've forgotten what it means to be kind. I cannot allow you to treat me this way. I have to let you go. I must care for myself now."

With a wave of her hand, the cage around the toad opened. For a moment, the toad stared at her in shock.

Then, with a croak of fury, he hopped away into the night and disappeared.

Adianna left the garden deep in thought. She realized that the gardener was right—her caring for the toad had come at the cost of her own well-being. She had forgotten to care for herself.

A New Beginning

With the toad gone, Adianna felt lighter. For the first time in weeks, she smiled—a real, joyful smile. She no longer felt small or trapped. She had learned that true kindness meant that taking care of herself was just as important as taking care of others.

Adianna never saw the gardener again, he was gone. From time to time, she would stop and ask herself if he was real or just a part of her imagination.

Whatever the case was, her heart was full of peace and his words stayed with her: "If your kindness does not include being kind to yourself, then you are incomplete."

Whatever the case was, her heart was full of peace and his words stayed with her: "If your kindness does not include being kind to yourself, then you are incomplete."

Adianna returned to her duties as princess, surrounded by her family and friends, knowing that she had the strength to care for others and herself, in equal measure.

And from that day on, the story of Princess Adianna and the Toad became a legend on the island of Ekuo—a tale of kindness, boundaries, and learning to let go.

LADY SIMONE PRINCESS ADIANNA'S LADY-IN-WAITING
AND GOOD FRIEND SAYS THAT THERE ARE SOME NEW
WORDS FROM THIS BOOK FOR YOU TO LEARN

✓ WRITE THEM DOWN
✓ LEARN HOW TO SPELL THEM
✓ FIND OUT WHAT THEY MEAN

BOUNDARIES ....

BOUGAINVILLEA...

CHIDED..

FAMILIAR..

HIBISCUS ....

LADY -IN-WAITING ....

PONDERING...

TINCTURE...

LADY SIMONE ALSO WANTS YOU TO FINISH THE NEXT
FEW SENTENCES SAYING ONLY GOOD THINGS ABOUT
YOURSELF WHILE YOU LOOK IN A MIRROR

I AM ....

I CAN ....

I WILL ....

LADY SIMONE HAS SOME QUESTIONS FOR YOU TO ANSWER ABOUT THE BOOK

1. Kindness to Others and Kindness to Yourself

At first, Adianna thought the toad needed help, but later he started being mean and asking for too much. Have you ever had a friend who wanted too much from you?

2. Recognizing Toxic Relationships

How can you tell if a friendship isn't making you feel good anymore?

3. Making Your Own Boundaries

Boundaries are like invisible lines that protect our feelings. How can you let people know when something doesn't feel okay to you?

4. The Power of Saying 'No'

When Adianna told the toad it was time for him to leave, she felt strong again. Have you ever felt scared to stand up for yourself and say 'NO' to someone?

5. Believing in Yourself?

Adianna learned that her happiness was just as important as taking care of others. What are some ways you can remind yourself that you matter too?

Princess Adianna and Lady Simone ask that you tell us how you liked the book.

It's called Leaving a Review.

Can you do that?

You can do this on Amazon.

Who knows maybe we can write another book for you if you give us some ideas.

Thank You